WHEATON PUBLIC LIBRARY
E Wahl
Wahl, Jan.   1967
Christmas in the forest

W9-BFQ-344

Christmas   142295
E
Wahl
Christmas in the forest

glued 12/89

Wheaton Public Library
225 N. Cross
Wheaton, Illinois 60187

PRINTED IN U.S.A.

CHRISTMAS IN THE FOREST

CHRISTMAS IN THE FOREST

By Jan Wahl · Pictures by Eleanor Schick

MACMILLAN PUBLISHING CO., INC.
NEW YORK

Copyright © Jan Wahl 1967
Copyright © Eleanor Schick 1967
All rights reserved. No part of this book may be
reproduced or transmitted in any form or by any means,
electronic or mechanical, including photocopying,
recording or by any information storage and retrieval
system, without permission in writing from the Publisher.
Macmillan Publishing Co., Inc.
866 Third Avenue, New York, N. Y. 10022
Collier-Macmillan Canada, Ltd., Toronto, Ontario
Library of Congress catalog card number: 67-17215
Printed in the United States of America
4   5   6   7   8   9   10

For Hansi Shoop with love

142295

All was hushed in the forest
on the animals' Christmas.

The elephant brought a great fir
from far away.

A red cardinal flew through the trees
carrying the news
The fir is here, The fir is here.

The llamas and the goats
who were slow of thinking,
thought,
We already have our fur.

The wolf helped the red deer,
whose antlers had caught
upon low-hanging branches.

Silently they walked together,
joined by the badger
and a family of foxes—
guided by bats who whistled soft carols.

Squirrels told stories, chattering low,
of the time the first Christmas came
announced by the ringing
of clear crystal bells.

Now, as it happened before,
the lion lay down with the lamb.

They gathered, one by one . . .
There was no
growling, howling, meowling
anywhere.

It was
hushed in the forest,
hushed, hushed, hushed, hushed.

The kangaroos picked cones and leaves
to hang on the branches.
The tiger strung berries on a string.

The antelope chewed the grass,
making a smooth lawn
for the fir.
The baboons painted the pine cones carefully.

The monkeys put the ornaments on.

And the giraffe laid, at the top, a star.

Then the tree was ready.
The animals gathered
in the silvery moonlight.

The raccoon lit the candles.
Darkness fell. However
no one moved.

Now up in the sky there appeared

a great constellation of bright shiny stars.

The bear said he was sure it was
a large and little bear.

While the tiger was sure it was
a large and little tiger.

Then a delicate golden glitter
flashed—

and each in that moment
made his quiet wish.

Walnuts and apricots, chestnuts and plums,
were dropped

by the cardinal's brothers and sisters
with a rustle of whirring wings.

The beautiful fir stood flickering all night.

And they danced—
they danced—they danced
until it was light of morning.